CIP Data is available.

Published in the United States 2001 by Dutton Children's Books,
a division of Penguin Putnam Books for Young Readers
345 Hudson Street, New York, New York 10014
www.penguinputnam.com

Originally published in Great Britain 2001 by Hamish Hamilton Ltd, London
Typography by Carolyn T. Fucile
Printed in China
First American Edition
ISBN 0-525-46661-4
2 4 6 8 10 9 7 5 3 1

GOOD DOG, DAISY!

LISA KOPPER

Dutton Children's Books ✦ NEW YORK

Daisy has three puppies: Morris,
Dolores, and Little Daisy.

Little Daisy is Baby's favorite puppy.

Baby likes to tell Little Daisy what to do.
Baby says, "SIT!" and Little Daisy sits.

Baby says, "LIE DOWN!"
and Little Daisy lies down.

Baby says, "SPEAK!"

And Little Daisy speaks: "SQUEAK!"

Here comes Daisy.

Baby sits.

And Baby lies down.

And Baby speaks: "WHAAAAA!"

Here comes Mommy.

Mommy says, "SIT, DAISY!"
But Daisy doesn't sit.

Mommy pushes on Daisy's bottom.
But Daisy doesn't sit.

Mommy sits.

And Mommy lies down.

And Mommy speaks:
"BAD DOG, DAISY!"

Then Mommy says,
"Come on, everybody. Get up."

...And everybody does.

GOOD DOG, DAISY!